USING THIS BOOK

One of the best ways of helping children learn to read is to read stories to them and with them. This way they learn what **reading** *is, and they will gradually come to recognize many words and begin to read for themselves.*

First, read the story on the left-hand pages aloud to the child.

Reread the story as often as the child enjoys hearing it. Talk about the pictures as you go.

Later the child will be able to read the words under the pictures on the right-hand pages.

The pages at the back of the book will give you some ideas for helping your child to read.

The Vanishing Monster

written by SHEILA McCULLAGH
illustrated by MARK CHADWICK

This book belongs to:

Ladybird Books

Davy lived in Puddle Lane.
He had a sister, whose name
was Sarah.

Davy

There was a big, old house
at the end of the lane.

The house was empty, and it had
a big garden.

Nobody minded if children went
into the garden to play.

the old house

One day, Davy pushed open the iron gate,
and went into the garden.
The sun was shining
and the sky was blue.
It was very hot.
Davy sat down under an old tree.

Davy sat down.

Davy had been sitting there
for a long time,
when he heard a noise.
He looked up and saw two long,
green ears.

Davy saw
two green ears.

Davy sat very still.
He kept very quiet.
Soon, he saw two green eyes.

Davy saw
two green eyes.

Davy sat very still.
He kept very quiet.
Soon, he saw a long green tail.

Davy saw
a long green tail.

Davy was just a little bit frightened.
But he kept very quiet,
and he sat very still.
The ears and the eyes and the tail
all joined up together,
and a big, green monster
came out of the bushes!

the green monster

At that moment, Davy sneezed.
He couldn't help it.
The sneeze burst out.
"Ah-choo!"

In a moment, the monster had vanished!

Davy didn't see him go.
He just wasn't there any more.
Davy stared.
The monster had gone.

The monster had gone.

Davy waited.

(He didn't feel frightened any more.)

Before long, he saw two green ears.

Davy saw
two green ears.

Then he saw two green eyes.
And then he saw a long, green tail.

Davy saw
two green eyes,
and a green tail.

The ears and the eyes and
the tail all joined up together.

The monster was back!
He looked very nervous.

The monster was back.

"Please don't be afraid, monster,"
said Davy. "I won't hurt you."

The monster jumped.
For a moment, Davy thought
that he would vanish again.
But he didn't.
He spoke in a whiffly-griffly voice.

"And I won't hurt **you**,"
said the monster.

Davy and the monster

"Who are you?" asked Davy.

"I'm a Griffle," said the monster,
in his whiffly-griffly voice.

"What's a Griffle?" asked Davy.

"A Griffle is a vanishing monster,"
said the Griffle. "Griffles are
always being frightened by people,
so they always vanish,
when they see anyone.
But I don't think I'm frightened
of **you**."

the Griffle

"Please don't be frightened of me,"
said Davy. "Stay here in the garden,
and play with me."

So the Griffle stayed,
and played with Davy.

Davy and the Griffle

They played hide-and-seek.
The Griffle was very good
at hiding. All he had to do,
was vanish.
But he always left his ears showing,
so that Davy could see him.

Davy saw
the green ears.

At last it was time for Davy
to go home.

"Please come with me,"
he said to the Griffle.
"I'd like you to come and stay."

"Are you sure you're not frightened?"
asked the Griffle.

"I'm not a bit frightened,"
said Davy.

So Davy and the Griffle went out
of the garden together.
They went back to Davy's house.

Davy and the Griffle
went back to
Davy's house.

As they got to the door
of Davy's house,
Davy's sister, Sarah, ran out.

"Hello, Davy," she cried.
"Where have you been?"

"Ssh!" said Davy.
"You'll frighten the Griffle."

Sarah ran out.

"What's a Griffle?" asked Sarah.

"He's a monster," said Davy.
"But he gets frightened very easily."

And when Davy looked,
the Griffle had vanished.

"He's gone," Davy said sadly.
"The Griffle was my friend,
and he's gone."

The monster had gone.

"There's nothing there," said Sarah.
"You must be making it up."

"I'm not," said Davy.
"He was here.
He played with me
in the garden.
I wish he hadn't gone."

"Maybe he'll come back," said Sarah.

The monster had gone.

Notes for the parent/teacher

When you have read the story, go back to the beginning. Look at each picture and talk about it. Point to the caption below, and read it aloud yourself. Run your finger under the words as you read, so that the child learns that reading goes from left to right. (You don't have to say this in so many words.

Children learn many useful things about reading just by reading with you, and it is often better to let them learn by experience rather than by explanation.)

The next time you go through the book, encourage the child to read the words and sentences under the illustrations. Don't

Mrs Pitter-Patter dropped the tail with a yell. She made such a noise, that she woke Mr Gotobed, who was fast asleep in bed in the house at the end of the lane.

Mr.Gotobed woke up.

rush in with a word before he* has time to think, but don't leave him struggling for too long. Always encourage him to feel that he is reading successfully, praising him when he does well, and avoiding criticism.

Now turn back to the beginning, and print the child's name in the space on the title page, using ordinary, not capital letters. Let him watch you print it: this is another useful experience.

*Children enjoy hearing the same story many times. Read this one as often as the child likes hearing it. The more opportunities he has to look at the illustrations and **read** the captions with you, the more he will come to recognize the words. Don't worry if he **remembers** rather than **reads** the captions. This is a normal stage in learning.*

If you have a number of books, let the child choose which story he would like to hear again.

---

* In order to avoid the continual "he or she," "him or her," the child is referred to in this book as "he." However, the stories are equally appropriate for boys and girls.

Have you read these stories about the cats and the Magician?

from Tim Catchamouse